A Day with My Aunt

Written By Marguerite Lynn Trupiano
Illustrated By Laurie Necco

RoseDog 🐾 Books

PITTSBURGH, PENNSYLVANIA 15222

ISBN: 978-1-4349-8126-4
eISBN: 978-1-4349-4369-9

Printed in the United States of America

First Printing

For information or to order additional books, please write:
RoseDog Books
701 Smithfield St.
Pittsburgh, PA 15222
U.S.A.
1-800-834-1803
www.rosedogbookstore.com

This book is dedicated to my family, especially Amber.

Thank you for always believing in me!

Dreams do come true.

Dad, I know you're my guardian angel watching over me...

Love you all. XOXO M.T.

For my mom, who always knew this would happen. L.N.

Hi! I'm Amber Rose and I'm going out on the town with my Aunt Lisa.

First, I have to do a few things. My mom has to give me a bubble bath so I can smell nice and clean.

After I get out of the tub I dry off and get
dressed. I have to wear my new pink outfit.

Mom was busy cooking breakfast in the kitchen.
She made waffles, I love to eat them with lots
of syrup!

I hear a car, I think it's my Aunt. The door bell rang, and it was Aunt Lisa! She had a list of surprises for us to do. I kissed my mom goodbye, and off we went.

I jumped in the back seat and put on my seat-
belt. I reminded Aunt Lisa to put hers on also.
As we backed down the driveway I couldn't wait
to hear the plan.

Aunt Lisa said, "close your eyes and count to ten. When we get to 10 we will be at one of your favorite places!" So I closed my eyes and counted...

I opened my eyes and we were at the Island Zoo!
We quickly parked the car and entered the Zoo.

First, I went on a pony ride. It was lots of fun. I was happy to see Patches the pony. He's the cutest pony in the whole zoo. He has pretty black hair and two white patches on his eyes. That's why they call him "Patches."

My Aunt gave me a dollar and I bought some crackers to feed the llamas, goats and sheep.

They were really hungry. The sheep came right up to the fence and took my last cracker. That's when it was time to move on to the next adventure!

Next, we went to see the reptiles and fish. It was really dark and scary. There was a big white sand shark that was so still it looked fake.

In the next tank there were two fish that looked like Nemo and Dory.

My Aunt said, "look at this giant anaconda snake." The anaconda looked right at me!

So I grabbed my Aunt's hand and slipped out the back door. What a relief, it was still sunny and bright outside!

My stomach was making funny noises, it was time to eat lunch.

We waved goodbye to the animals and left the zoo.

My Aunt asked me where I want to eat lunch? I said "Hamburger Palace."
"That's exactly where I want to go", said Aunt Lisa.

We drove to Hamburger Palace and ordered 2 hamburgers and french fries. It was an awesome day.

"What's next?" I asked. My Aunt said, "close your eyes and count to 10." So I closed my eyes and counted

1, 2, 3, 4, 5, 6, 7, 8, 9, 10!

We were at Spider Park. Yeah! I love to go to the park. Spider Park has the best swings and slide in all of Staten Island.

My Aunt had some rules before I went to play.
No running off, no talking to strangers, take turns
and don't be a hog on the swings.

We had so much fun! My Aunt raced me down the slide...

...And we played on the swings.

I started to get tired, so we headed home. When we reached the front door I could hardly keep my eyes open.

I thanked my aunt for a great day and hugged her goodbye.

As I climbed on the couch mommy wanted to hear all about my day.

I started to tell her to count to 10....

....and my eyes became very sleepy.
I started to count with her.

1, 2, 3, 4, ...

. . . . ZZZZZZZZ

Printed by Publishers' Graphics LLC
PGD-07035